BEE TREE

DRAGON'S LAIR

OWL'S HOUSE

CHRISTOPHER ROBIN'S HOUSE

EEYORE'S GLOOMY PLACE

Pooh's Very Own First Book

Walt Disney
Productions'

Pooh's Very Own First Book

Golden Press • New York
Western Publishing Company, Inc.
Racine, Wisconsin

CONTENTS

Names and More Names

Christopher Robin and his friends can spell their names.
Can you spell your name?

TiGGER

KANGA

RABBiT

DRAGON

Roo

OWL

CHRISTOPHER ROBIN

Very
Small
Beetle

POOH EEYORE

rian

PIGLET

7

The Alphabet

A

Acorn

B

Balloon

C

Custard

Daisy

D

Egg

E

Fish

F

9

G

Galoshes

H

Honey

I

Ivy

Jacket

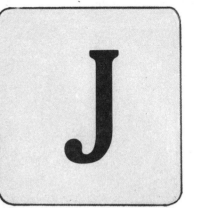

J

Kite

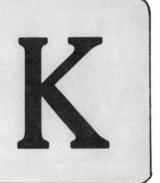

K

Lunch

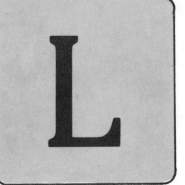

L

M

Mud

N

Nap

O

Owl

Pooh and Piglet

P

Quilt

Q

Raking

R

S

T

U

V

Stripes

Thistles

Umbrella

Vegetables

Writing

W

Xylophone

X

Yo-Yo

Y

Zipper

Z

15

Counting Is Fun

Roo can count up to twenty. Can you?

1

ONE lonely Eeyore

2

TWO balloons for Roo

3

THREE pots of honey (and one happy bear)

4

FOUR flying feet

5

FIVE crunchy carrots

17

6

SIX friendly faces

7

SEVEN pots of honey (and one happy bear)

8

EIGHT favorite flowers

9

NINE of Rabbit's friends-and-relations

10

TEN falling leaves

11

ELEVEN thistles for Eeyore

12

TWELVE of Kanga's cookies

13

THIRTEEN shiny swords

14

FOURTEEN fluffy tails

15

FIFTEEN of Owl's quill pens

16
SIXTEEN soft snowflakes

17
SEVENTEEN clover blossoms

18
EIGHTEEN buzzing bees

19
NINETEEN fat footprints

20
TWENTY pots of honey
(and one happy bear)

23

Let's Play School

It's time for school and Christopher Robin is the teacher. Here are some questions Christopher Robin is going to ask his class. Can you answer them?

1. Piglet, what is the first letter of the alphabet?
   (You can find the answer on page 8 of this book.)

2. What is the last letter of the alphabet, Rabbit?
   (The answer is on page 15.)

3. Pooh, how many pupils are there in this schoolroom?
   (Pooh knows he must not count Christopher Robin because he is the teacher.)

4. What letter does your name begin with, Owl?
   (In case you can't remember, the answer is on page 12.)

5. Tigger, how many feet do you bounce with?
   (If you need to look up the answer, it's on page 17.)

Seasons

In Spring . . .

Christopher Robi
walks in the rain.

Kanga cleans house.

Rabbit plants
a garden.

Pooh
picks flowers.

And Tigger bounces as usual.

In Summer . . .

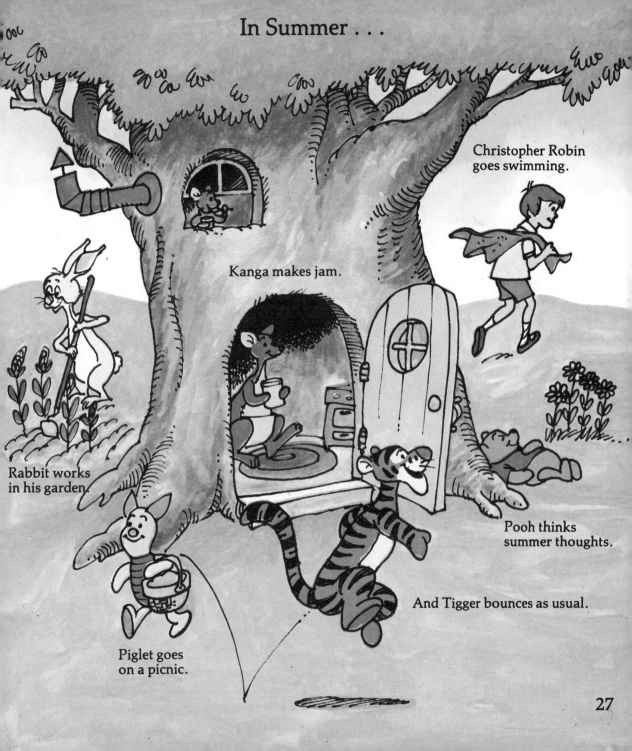

Christopher Robin goes swimming.

Kanga makes jam.

Rabbit works in his garden.

Pooh thinks summer thoughts.

And Tigger bounces as usual.

Piglet goes on a picnic.

27

In Fall . . .

Christopher Robin picks apples.

Pooh goes to school.

Rabbit rakes leaves.

And Tigger bounces as usual.

Piglet collects acorns.

28

In Winter . . .

Pooh sleeps by the fire.

Kanga knits sweaters.

Christopher Robin goes sledding.

Roo and Piglet build a snowman.

And Tigger bounces as usual.

29

Colors, Colors Everywhere

Christopher Robin, Pooh, and Piglet are having fun in the Hundred Acre Wood. Can you find all the things on this page that are RED?

Rabbit has come to visit Owl. There are 10 YELLOW things in Owl's house. Can you name them?

It's raining today, so some of Rabbit's young relations are staying indoors. Can you find 8 ORANGE things in Rabbit's house?

Winnie-the-Pooh is ready for bed. It is one of his favorite times. And BLUE is one of his very favorite colors. How many BLUE things can you find in his bedroom?

Kanga has cooked a wonderful dinner for Roo. There are 8 GREEN things in her kitchen. Can you find them?

Piglet and Tigger have come to visit Eeyore in his Gloomy Place. There are 5 PURPLE things on this page. Can you find them? (Hint: One is Eeyore's favorite!)

All Kinds of Sizes

Christopher Robin is *tall*.

Kanga is *big*.

Piglet is *short*.

Roo is *little*.

Eeyore's ears are *long*.

Pooh's ears are *short*.

Rabbit is *thin*.

Sir Brian is *fat*.

Christopher Robin is the *biggest.*

Dragon is *bigger* . . .

Pooh is *big* . . .

Rabbit's friends-and-relations are

small . . .

smaller . . .

smallest . . .

and
teeny-weeny.

All Kinds of Shapes

This is a *circle*.
It is round like Pooh's balloon.
The wheels on Pooh's wagon are round.
The buttons on Christopher Robin's jacket are round, too.
Can you find any other round things on this page?

This is a *square*.
Sir Brian's window is square.
So is the picture on the wall.
The checkerboard has lots of squares.
Can you find any other square shapes on this page?

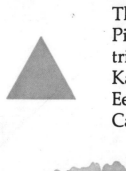

This is a *triangle*.
Piglet is playing an instrument that's called a triangle because of its shape.
Kanga's and Roo's hats are shaped like triangles.
Eeyore's flag is a triangle, too.
Can you find any other triangles on this page?

This is a *rectangle*.
Pooh is sitting at a table that is a rectangle.
The napkins on the table are rectangles, too.
Can you find any other rectangles on this page?

Kanga has an egg. It is *oval*.

There is a new moon over Owl's head. It is *crescent*-shaped.

Piglet is flying a kite. It is shaped like a *diamond*.

Rabbit is giving Eeyore a *heart*-shaped valentine.

Christopher Robin is wearing
a badge shaped like a *star*.

Pooh is drawing a *straight* line.

Now Pooh is drawing a *curved* line.

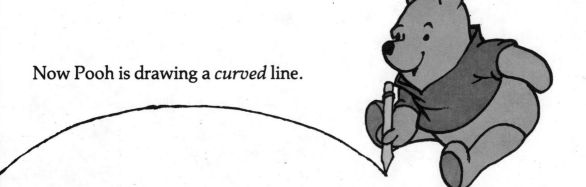

Hide-and-Seek

Pooh and his friends are playing hide-and-seek in the Hundred Acre Wood. Piglet is trying to find everyone. Can you help him find his friends?

All Kinds of Weather

Rain, rain, rain!

Christopher Robin puts on his hat, his boots, and his raincoat. He gets his umbrella. He's going for a walk in the rain.

Owl likes to stay where it is nice and dry. He is looking at his favorite picture book.

What do you like to do on a rainy day?

On sunny days Rabbit loves to be outside with his friends-and-relations.

"Sunny days are good fishing days," says Rabbit.

"They're also good lazy days," says Very Small Beetle.

What do you like to do on sunny days?

49

On a blustery day, the wind swooshes through the trees of the Hundred Acre Wood. It blows leaves from the trees.

Piglet likes to fly his kite on a windy day.

What do you like to do on windy days?

Poor Eeyore! The wind has blown part of his house down.

The Six Pine Trees look beautiful in the snow. Have you ever seen a snowflake up close? It looks like a piece of lace.

Pooh likes to make tracks in the new snow. Then he turns around to see where he's been.

What do you like to do on a snowy day?

Opposites

Owl is *up.*

Pooh is *down.*

How many UP-in-the-sky things can you find?
How many DOWN-on-the-ground things do you see?

Roo is *in*.

Roo is *out*.

Rabbit is *hot*. As soon as he has finished his work, he is going to have a glass of *cold* lemonade.

Piglet is *cold*. He is hoping Kanga will have a cup of *hot* chocolate waiting for him.

Eeyore is *slow*.

Tigger is *fast*.

Tigger bounces *high*.

Eeyore keeps his head *low*.

Tigger likes
to bounce *over* things.

Very Small Beetle likes
to crawl *under* things.

Owl flies *over*
the Six Pine Trees.

Pooh stands *under*
his favorite bee tree.

56

Piglet's Piggy Bank

Christopher Robin gave Piglet a piggy bank on his birthday. It looked a lot like Piglet.

"It's very nice," said Piglet admiringly. "Thank you, Christopher Robin."

"But what is it for?" asked Pooh who had dropped by to wish Piglet a happy birthday.

"Silly old bear," Christopher Robin said. "You put money in it—in the little slot between the ears."

"It's a good way to save your pennies, nickels, dimes, and quarters," said Christopher Robin.

Pooh and Piglet looked so puzzled that Christopher Robin decided then and there to teach them about money.

He reached into his pocket and showed Pooh and Piglet the money he had. He had five pennies, two nickels, two dimes, and one quarter.

He explained to Piglet and Pooh:

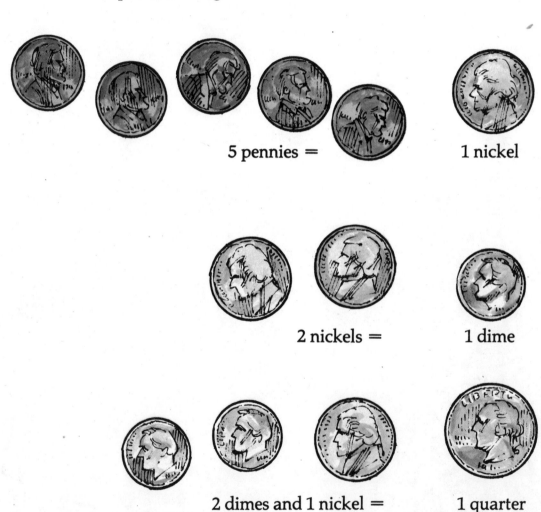

5 pennies =   1 nickel

2 nickels =   1 dime

2 dimes and 1 nickel =   1 quarter

"Thank you, Christopher Robin," said Pooh.
"Now I know about money."
"Me, too," said Piglet proudly.
Christopher Robin gave Piglet a nickel and a dime
to put in his piggy bank. Piglet was so pleased.

Pooh's Honey-Hiding Places

Pooh is always afraid that he will run out of honey, so he keeps an extra supply tucked away in many secret places. Can you find all the honey pots he has hidden?

Houses in the Hundred Acre Wood

There are different kinds of houses in the Hundred Acre Wood. Pooh and Piglet have houses in trees. Dragon's home is a cave and Sir Brian's home is a castle.

Here are all the houses in the Hundred Acre Wood.

Pooh's House (It has a bell above the door.)

Piglet's House (It's close to Pooh's house.)

Kanga's House (Roo lives here and
Tigger does, too.)

Christopher Robin's House (Don't you
like the swing?)

Owl's House (It is the highest
house of them all.)

65

Rabbit's House (There are spare rooms for Rabbit's many relations.)

Eeyore's House (It is in a sad and gloomy place.)

Dragon's House (He calls it his lair,
but when he lettered the sign he spelled it "liar.")

Sir Brian's House (It has a moat and drawbridge.)

Everyone in the Hundred Acre Wood wants you to see inside his house, or at least a favorite room. Here they are:

Pooh's favorite room is where his honey cupboard is located.

Piglet likes his playroom best.

Rabbit has a room where he keeps all his garden tools.

Christopher Robin likes the room with the window where he can look out over the Hundred Acre Wood.

Kanga's favorite room is her kitchen.

Owl is very proud of his library.

Sir Brian's favorite room is where
he keeps his armor and shield.

Dragon likes his dark room for thinking.

Eeyore doesn't have a favorite room. Wouldn't you know!

Very Small Beetle's
favorite room
is under a leaf.

If you lived in the Hundred Acre Wood,
which house would you want to be yours?

Pooh's Poems

Pooh loves to make up poems:
Tum-tum-de-dum, Tum-tum-de-dum,
Making up poems about honey is fun.

He makes up a good morning poem:
Good morning! Good morning!
The day is so sunny.
For breakfast, for breakfast,
I think I'll have honey.

He makes up a noon day poem:
The sun's high in the sky,
I know that it's noon,
It's time for a snack;
Where's my honey and spoon?

He makes up an evening poem:
The day is done.
I've done a lot.
It's time to get
My honey pot!

Can you make up a poem for Pooh to say?

Christopher Robin's Band

Christopher Robin is the leader of the Hundred Acre Wood Band. The band is practicing for a concert they will give soon.

Pooh goes oomp-pah-pah on the tuba.

Owl goes hoot and toot on the trombone.

Piglet plays the piccolo.

Eeyore beats the drum.

Rabbit strums the guitar.

Dragon plays the trumpet.

Kanga plays the piano while Roo turns the pages.

Sir Brian plays the saxophone.

Tigger crashes the cymbals.

Christopher Robin, baton in hand, leads the band.

Favorite Things

Favorite things are things you like very much. Everyone in the Hundred Acre Wood has favorite foods, toys, flowers, colors, smells, and favorite things to do.

What are your "favorites"?

Here is Piglet flying his favorite kite.

Here's Pooh with his favorite balloon.

Tigger's favorite thing to do is bouncing.

What Rabbit likes best is to play hide-and-seek.

When it comes to favorite times,
Pooh votes for breakfast time
and lunchtime and suppertime,
not to mention snack time.
Pooh's favorite food is honey.

Rabbit thinks carrots are
the best food there is.

Piglet likes acorns.
He calls them "haycorns."

And Dragon adores
toasted marshmallows.

77

Eeyore's favorite flower is a purple thistle. He likes to smell them and to eat them, too.

Kanga is in her flower garden trying to decide which flower is her favorite. She likes them all, but she thinks the roses smell best.

Sir Brian and Dragon agree that fighting each other is their favorite sport. They always take turns about winning.

Dragon's hat is his very favorite piece of clothing.

Sir Brian polishes his favorite armor to keep it from getting rusty.

Everyone in the Hundred Acre Wood agrees that visiting Christopher Robin is a very favorite thing to do. Christopher Robin likes to have everyone get very comfortable. Then he serves them his favorite drink—hot chocolate.

What Shall We Wear Today?

Pooh and his friends in the Hundred Acre Wood don't worry much about what they wear. Christopher Robin, however, has clothing for warm weather, cold weather, dry weather, wet weather, and special days.

On rainy days, Christopher Robin wears his raincoat, his rain hat, and his rain boots. He also carries his umbrella, which is large enough to keep most of his friends dry.

What do you wear on rainy days?

On wintry, snowy days, Christopher Robin puts on an
extra sweater. He wraps a scarf around his neck before he
snuggles into his heavy coat. He pulls his stocking cap down
over his ears. His mittens keep his hands warm. Sometimes
his feet get cold even when he wears snow boots.

How do you dress in wintertime?

In summer, when Christopher Robin goes to the beach, he wears sandals and swimming trunks. And he takes along a big beach towel.

For picnics in the Hundred Acre Wood, Christopher Robin wears shorts, a T-shirt, and sneakers.

Pooh doesn't care much what he wears, but he always watches to see if someone is carrying a picnic basket and if there's at least one pot of honey in it.

What Can You Remember?

Christopher Robin was talking to his friends in the Hundred Acre Wood. "Remembering is fun," he told them. "Can you think back to important things that happened to you?" Everyone started thinking back.

"Can you remember which birthday party was the best?" he asked.

Pooh thought it might have been his last one, or the one before.

"Who was your first best friend?" Christopher Robin asked.

Tigger said everyone was his best friend.

Eeyore wanted to know who could remember a sad time.
He said his favorite sad time was when he lost his tail.
(But Pooh found it for him.)

The best glad time that Piglet could remember
was when he was given his first kite.

Can you remember:

A visit to a faraway place

Your first favorite food

A special toy

Your first favorite story

A time when you were afraid

A time when you were sick

Think hard. How far back can you remember?

Parts of the Body

Winnie-the-Pooh posed for this poster. It's to help everyone name the parts of the body:

(Front View)　　　　　　　　(Back View)

Come to the Fair

Christopher Robin surprised everyone in the Hundred Acre Wood. He took them to the fair, which was being held just across the stream and down the road from his house.

Everyone had a wonderful time. But Tigger bounced too high and lost his ice cream.

QUILTS

Pooh at Work

Pooh is very busy. He has certain jobs to do, and he helps others, too.

Empty honey pots have to be washed.

He picks a pretty bouquet of flowers.

The table must be set for lunch.

He sweeps the floor.

Do you have jobs to do?

Pooh helps Kanga carry groceries.

He shakes down the acorns
so Piglet can pick them up.

Pooh helps Rabbit hoe his garden.

He brings Eeyore some
freshly picked thistles.

Do you help others?

Pooh at Play

Pooh likes playtime best of all.

Flying a kite is lots of fun.

He likes puzzles, especially on rainy days.

Jogging is good for a bear of some stoutness.

Pooh plays hide-and-seek all by himself. He hides his honey pots and then he finds them.

Pooh and Piglet play hopscotch.

Pooh plays follow-the-leader
with Rabbit and his friends-and-relations.

Pooh, Piglet, and Roo
build a snowman. Does it
look like anybody you know?

A good party game is
"Pin the Tail on the Donkey,"
but not on Eeyore!

Good-bye